The Beauty of Nature

By Andrea Posner-Sanchez
Illustrated by Elisa Marrucchi

Random House 🏠 New York

ISBN: 978-0-7364-2771-5
www.randomhouse.com/kids
Printed in the United States of America
10 9 8 7 6 5 4 3 2 1

$\mathcal{P}$rincesses are as kind to nature as they are to people. They love to tend their gardens, care for animals, and keep the world green and healthy.

Snow White makes sure the Seven Dwarfs don't waste water when they wash up for dinner.

Tiana turns off the lights when she leaves a room.

Jasmine picks up any litter she finds.

Cinderella plants a tree. Trees help keep the air clean.

Ariel finds ways to reuse things instead of throwing them away.
This seaweed makes a lovely scarf.

Belle uses both sides of the paper when she writes letters.

Tiana cooks with fresh fruits and vegetables grown right in her own backyard.

Snow White is always kind to animals.

Belle tells the shopkeeper she doesn't need a bag for her new books.

Cinderella turns her old clothes into new ones for her little friends.

Be kind to our world—and you'll be like a princess, too!